GUSTAVE GUICHES

THE MODESTY OF SODOM

TRANSLATED AND WITH AN INTRODUCTION BY
BRIAN STABLEFORD

THIS IS A SNUGGLY BOOK

ISBN: 978-1-64525-042-5

THE MODESTY OF SODOM

GUSTAVE GUICHES (1860-1935) was a native of the French department of the Lot. After passing the final examinations entitling him to practice law in 1880 he decided instead to dedicate himself to literature. Like many pillars of the nascent Decadent Movement, he frequented Charles Buet's salon, made useful acquaintances there, and soon began to publish poems and short stories in periodicals. Though best remembered for his 1888 novella *La Pudeur de Sodome*, he wrote numerous other works, including *Céleste Prudhomat* (1886), and *Au fil de la vie* (1895).

BRIAN STABLEFORD'S scholarly work includes *New Atlantis: A Narrative History of Scientific Romance* (Wildside Press, 2016), *The Plurality of Imaginary Worlds: The Evolution of French roman scientifique* (Black Coat Press, 2017) and *Tales of Enchantment and Disenchantment: A History of Faerie* (Black Coat Press, 2019). In support of the latter projects he has translated more than a hundred volumes of *roman scientifique* and more than twenty volumes of *contes de fées* into English.

His recent fiction, in the genre of metaphysical fantasy, includes a trilogy of novels set in West Wales, consisting of *Spirits of the Vasty Deep* (2018), *The Insubstantial Pageant* (2018) and *The Truths of Darkness* (2019), published by Snuggly Books.

CONTENTS

INTRODUCTION

LA PUDEUR DE SODOM by Gustave Guiches, here translated as "The Modesty of Sodom," was originally published in *La Revue indépendante*, then edited by Édouard Dujardin and Téodor de Wyzewa, in 1888; it was subsequently reprinted as a small booklet in the same year by Quantin. It had been preceded in the periodical in 1887 by an earlier story, "Les Ombres gardiennes," here translated as "The Guardian Shades," and included as a makeweight. *La Pudeur de Sodom* achieved an instant notoriety by virtue of the sarcasm of its theme, which seemed to some readers to skirt blasphemy, not so much against the Lord, although his representation in the story as a character is certainly a trifle irreverent, but against the city of Paris, symbolized within the story as the city of Sodom.

By 1888 the Symbolist Movement was in full swing in Paris, allied since the advent of the label with the accusation of decadence. First applied by hostile journalists as an insult leveled against a perceived literary *avant garde,* the "decadent" label was immediately taken up by some members of that aspirant *avant garde* as a triumphant proclamation, exactly as it had been fifty years earlier by some writers associated with the Romantic Movement, who took a paradoxically perverse delight in being thought to be "decadent." The term had achieved an apotheosis of sorts when it was adopted, teasingly, by Théophile Gautier in his essay introducing the collected works of Charles Baudelaire—the hero and role-model of all self-proclaimed decadent writers—which dutifully denied the applicability of the term before going on to redefine the "Decadent style" in an elaborate and laudatory fashion, in a passage that became a key reference point for would-be members of the new "Decadent Movement" of the 1880s.

As defined by Gautier, Decadent style is ornate, mannered and musical, drawing on a rich vocabulary in order to identify novel analogies;

it is, naturally, affiliated to Gautier's own ideology of "l'art pour l'art," translated into English as "art for art's sake," but Decadent poetry and prose has always retained a strong sarcastic fascination with the idea of "cultural decadence" popularized in France by Baron de Montesquieu and has frequently reveled in presenting images of that kind of decadence, mythically identified with such ancient cities as Babylon and such fictitious kings as Sardanapalus. One of the subtexts of Montesquieu's theory of historical repetition was that eighteenth-century France had entered fully into the epoch of its decadence, summarized and exemplified in the city of Paris and the Bourbon monarchy, and that the post-Revolutionary nineteenth century would be its inevitable aftermath—a prophesy as accurate as any in the Bible.

All of that is neatly and flamboyantly exemplified by *La Pudeur de Sodom*, one of the purest and most strident exercises of *fin-de-siècle* Decadent art. As well as employing colorful exotic terms, the author invents and improvises new ones freely, and the story contains several words found nowhere else, whose meanings have to be inferred from context or etymological analogies. The story is a straight-faced black comedy, as the majority of exercises in literary decadence are, and its humor is appropriately scathing in its aggressive but amused assault on moral hypocrisy; it is very much a product of its time, but one which, alas, has by no means lost all its relevance in the historical interim.

Gustave Guiches (1860-1935) was a native of the French department of the Lot, which might not be irrelevant to the choice of his theme in *La Pudeur de Sodom*, but after passing the final examinations entitling him to practice law in 1880 he decided instead to dedicate himself to literature—a pattern very commonplace among the writers of *fin-de-siècle* Paris—initially taking a day-job working for the gas company, procured for him by his brother-in-law. Like many pillars of the nascent Decadent Movement, including Barbey d'Aurevilly, Villiers de l'Isle Adam, Joris-Karl Huysmans, Léon Bloy and Jean Lorrain, he frequented Charles Buet's salon, made useful acquaintances there, and soon began to publish poems and short stories in periodicals.

With Paul Bonnetain, J.-H. Rosny. Lucien Descaves and Paul Margueritte, Guiches signed the "*Manifeste des cinq*" published in *Le Figaro* in 1887 as a rival to Jean Moréas Symbolist Manifesto, featured in the same newspaper the previous year, thus establishing himself as a renegade of sorts from Stéphane Mallarmé's conceptualization of literary Symbolism, and his alliance with the experimentally-inclined Dujardin and Wyzewa, who developed their own "Wagnerian" theory of art in a similar spirit, was entirely natural. He went on to enjoy a long and fruitful career as a novelist and playwright, again following a common pattern in gradually discarding his Symbolist and Decadent affectations while retaining an essential fundamental irony and dark humor in the world-view of his work. He undoubtedly considered his later work as more mature and polished—and rightly so—but in common with many other writers associated with the literary movements of the *fin-de-siècle*, readers and critics thought that it had lost a certain trenchant edge, a raw exuberance that is difficult to retain as youth matures. For that reason, *La Pudeur de Sodom* remained, and still remains, his most famous and most frequently-cited work, whose translation into English is long overdue.

"Les Ombres gardiennes" is a slight work by comparison, but it is an interesting exercise on the edge of the genre of the *fantastique*, of a kind that became particularly prevalent in the *fin-de-siècle*, which carefully retains a superficial ambiguity in its representation of its crucial incident. There are dozens of similar studies of madness and hallucination, which retain varying degrees of sympathy for the subjective supernatural interpretations imposed on events by their protagonists, and it is interesting to compare and contrast the story with Édouard Dujardin's many variations of the same theme collected in *Les Hantises* (1886; tr. as *Hauntings*). Its stylistic affectations, in juxtaposition with *La Pudeur de Sodom*, provide a graphic parenthetical illustration of the thematic breadth and scope of the Decadent Movement.

The translations were made from the relevant issues of *La Revue indépendante* preserved on the Bibliothèque Nationale's *gallica* website, the copy of the Quantin booklet scanned by the Hathi Trust being jealously protected from non-American eyes for occult "copyright reasons" even though the text is clearly in the public domain.

—Brian Stableford, March 2020.

THE MODESTY OF SODOM

Et exclamavit voce magna Susanna . . .
Clamaverunt autem et sens adversum eam

Daniel XIII:24[1]

---

1 The first line of this compound quote, which translates as "And Susanna cried out in a loud voice," recurs in a well-known Gregorian chant, but is taken from the Vulgate version of *Daniel* 13: 42-44; the improvised addendum suggests that her cry of protest had a different meaning from that understood. The story of Susanna, in which she is falsely accused of lewd behaviour by corrupt elders, is removed from many versions of the Bible because it is not in the presumed Hebrew original but was preserved in most French versions.

I

IN the fervor of the day, Abraham rested in the depths of the valley of Mamre, on the mats of shadow that the oaks wove to refresh the soil.

It was the dog-days of Abib. The centuries descended upon the patriarch healthily. Their ineffable hours drained away in his pastoral retreat, in the depths of his valley of abundance marvelous with luminous fertility. Everything material was dazzling. Vines and olive groves flowed over the two slopes of the besieged mountain in thick and luxuriant silver masses. The silence was a tender meditation of beings and things, assimilating the felicities that rained down upon them in solar cataracts. Here and there, fortunate noises fluttered around that contemplation numbed by enchantment: flocks of small birds, frolicsome sheaves of sparks, setting fire to the foliage of the gum-trees; the risible chirping of golden-winged blackbirds brightening the clumps of reeds with their whistling folly; the sighing prayers of pink turtle-doves weeping amorously at the turnings blued by the suave dusk; and even ripe gourds detached one by one from the fruit-trees of Sodom, crashing into the hyacinths, dissipating the smoke of their pips.

All those fruits were the delicious tremors of the silence. They celebrated the contentment purred by the methodical crunching of invisible jaws, the simultaneous rumination of swarming populations of livestock.

Up above, the splendors of the air were enthroned. Although resigned for many years only to see a tent of sky stitching its changing canvas over the crests of the mountains, Abraham's eyes were able to resuscitate the vastness of visions. With a single bound, his memory captured the Paradise of the altitudes.

Then his gaze launched forth into infinite esplanades of green-tinted blue. Claws clenched under the ebony cross of their glorious wings, soaring eagles impelled their sovereign ascents with oar-like thrusts. Cloudy ramparts fortified the extent. It chimerized the ideal heights as the humps of dromedaries, crouching sphinxes, obelisks of snow, isolated domes and caravans of hills, and the entire horizon was occupied by warrior encampments of mountains: a predestined horizon prophesying, amid the burning bushes of the sun, the exoduses and bounding escapes of the future.

Behold the mountains of Ephraim and Ieouda, rising up in confused stages on their flourishing foundations. The adamantine facets of the glaciers of Mount Hermon fulgurate, and the Lebanon of the Phoenicians and the Arameans fades away gently in the distance. Diaphanous mallows cloud its mystical slopes, saddled by cedars and crowned with roses. A volcano of essences bursts forth at the imperceptible summit. Fusing in sheaves, immediately volatilized, the eruption of aromatics saturates the breeze, and delectable manna disperses throughout space the vapor of the incense-burners of Lebanon. That dew, the earth, the trees, the plants and the flowers receive. It penetrates thirsty fleeces and is exhaled from the earth, the trees, the plants and the flowers. The kiss of the perfumes unites the vegetations seraphically. The gum-trees incense the turpentine trees. The tamarinds are etherized with benzoin. Gashed pines weep their odorous tears of resin, drop by drop, and pious canticles of myrrh are murmured by choirs of junipers.

Abraham said to himself that all those things were beautiful, and his rejoicing and his gratitude blossomed in his contemplation. Peace had pitched its tents in his soul, and amid the external delights it delighted equally in the beatitudes of his thought. Where now were the giant Nephilim? Where were the barbaric Enaquites and the sanguinary Zouzim, the monsters of buzzing confusion? The land was purified; it had the pacific magnificence of the atmosphere. Give thanks to the supreme organizer! Give thanks to the benevolent wings of Elohim! Glory to Yahveh! And the soul of the patriarch, reckless in adoration, knelt down in universal gratitude.

Cries of celebration rose in chorus, climbing the hills. Leaning his hand on the goatskin trailing on the ground, Abraham turned his gaze toward the place from which the joyful clamors were coming. It was in the valley of Rephaim, a rejoicing of pastors. His servant Elezer was watching all the ewes. Loading their slings with stones from their baskets, children were pursuing flocks of sparrows, and stones ricocheted from the heights. At that reminder of anniversary joys, the patriarch smiled. He turned toward his tent, not far away. Its door was closed by shadow. He saw an aged servant emerge who, lifting an earthenware vase by both handles, headed for the well. He told himself that all was well.

On a rocky spur on the crest of the mountain a camel perched its double hump with difficulty. Others followed, dotting the summits. The patriarch recognized the drivers, a caravan of Ammonite merchants, Doubtless they were laden with green fards of mesdjem,[1] painted robes, incense, aloes, myrrh and cinnamon. Brown and white, the camels filed, swollen with pride, their eyes vigilant in front of their ram-like heads. Behind trotted slender gazelles and alert donkeys harnessed with Phoenician crimson and bearing sacks swollen by the sand of the Belus.[2]

He watched the caravan shrink in the distance, the crimson still rutilant like a torch, finally immersed in the dust of the Sal-Aphot.[3]

---

1 "Dorin el Mesdjem" was a *fin-de-siècle* brand name primarily associated with jars of kohl.

2 The sands of the river Belus were famous in antiquity for their use in glass manufacture.

3 Sal-Aphot was a name given to a hot wind blowing from the eastern desert.

Then, as it finished disappearing, going in the direction of Egypt, a sudden cock-crow aroused his memories. The nomad woke up, indignant at his old age, his soul alert. No longer hearing anything but the "Forward ho!" that the Lord was clamoring in a formidable din of trumpets, he looked back and no longer found anything but the paltry years of his childhood comparable to the lassitude to which the idleness of siestas under the oaks of Mamre condemned him.

II

HE had no regrets for that childhood, so briefly sedentary and so vainly studious, stifled in Ur-Kasdim, where he built houses of brick, molded his words on clay and interpreted the course of the stars. To those frivolous occupations, only worthy of Chaldean scholars, he much preferred a matinal departure, to the sound of the trumpets gathering the flocks! The earth wept joy. The sky extended solar benedictions over all living things.

And everywhere, the capers of black he-goats and white lambs, the impetuous collisions of she-goats and the delirious gambols of rams. The jubilation of light! The salubrity of the air! The curiosity of unfamiliar veils of mist! The mirage of distant things that it is necessary to attain . . . !

Between the Garizin and the Ebak, here is the first halt in the sumptuous pasturage of Sichem, the climb over the lush hills. But the Lord's "Forward ho!" is ringing in the ears Decamp your flocks, lugging the gourds of their udders and shedding torrential wakes of milk.

Here is Chenaim, a dazzle of olive groves, fields gorged with pasture, the carbuncles of pomegranates, fig-trees abandoned to the embrace of clusters, the somber multiple prosperities of mulberries. March on! March on! The Lord's arms assign Space. The voice awakens echoes. March on!

The terrain disappears, scarcely glimpsed. The pastor bestrides it, always driving the lively crowds of livestock. They charge into the distance. The ground shakes. Hunters clad in bear-skins surge forth on the escarpments and, bows taut, are immobilized by stupor at the passage of that animal typhoon. Before encampments, children throw stones at the bulls of the advance guard. Terrified women gesticulate . . .

Here is the mount of Bethel. A halt. An altar is erected to the glory of Yahveh. The smoke of the sacrifice rises up in its votive column, grave and respected by the wind. But the Lord indicates the route and signifies new expanses.

March on! March on! Like cataracts of animals, the flocks tumble, plunging steeply over the plains, stampeding in panic as if under a flagellating rain of whiplashes. The guard-dogs gallop, biting the legs of laggards and multiplying their barking. March on!

For here is Hebron! And the voice no longer sounds its "Forward ho!" The silence of Heaven commands repose.

III

WHENCE comes that tumult of war? Abraham listens in the Past. He recognizes the din. The Sylvan Valley yawns in its wells of bitumen. It vibrates with the drumming of shields. Verminous hordes are swarming in its depths. Chodorlaomor, Thadal, Amraphol and Arioch are marching to encounter the king of Sodom and Gomorrah, who is fleeing, harassed by howling mobs of confederated warriors. Now, Abraham is astonished. He recalls that he obeyed the voice blindly, that he went forth like those men who walk in their sleep. His three hundred and eighteen servants and his three companions, Escol, Aner and Mambre, gather around him. Assyrians commanded by their powerful king Schoschannah have collapsed near Dan . . .

IV

WHAT is happening now? An illumination of glory. Magnanimous turbulence, august corteges of rhythm. Surrounded by his victorious troops, Abram awaits the honors. Horses prance, caparisoned in crimson. The atmosphere is radiant with coruscations of gold and precious stones. Bare-chested, hips striped with vermilion mesh of Schentis, arms circled by bracelets, beards and hair braided, the Sars of the Pentapolis, the sumptuous kings of Sodom, Gomorrah, Adamah, Zoar and Seboim advance. Before them, the Sheikh of Schalem, Malki-Zadek, ornamented with a Schimar mantle parted over his carapace of solar disks coiled in a uraeus whose heads reflect the glare of the sun . . . Behind them, tambourines of kinnor and asosta are being beaten furiously. Further behind, troops and booty heaped on the iron carts of the Canaanites, advance toward Abram . . .

V

B UT the Past is feminized. Amour arrives. That is Sara, the beautiful Chaldean, as slender as a gazelle, with the charming, submissive and passionate gaze. Is that not the clink of silver in the bracelets of her feet? She approaches from the wells where the livestock had gathered. Night falls, weary, swooning. Here, in the embalming of the acacias, behind the fan of aloes, is the hour of ecstasies and the plenitude of delights. How, in his jealousy, he disputes her by means of cunning with the Pharaoh of Egypt! How . . .

VI

B UT as well as Jealousy, Amour, Glory, Fortune, War and all the agitation of nomadic times collapses, is pulverized, volatilized, is annihilated, and of all those terrestrial things nothing subsists in Abraham but the supreme amour, the supreme reverence for the almighty God who had ordered them. All other reminiscences expelled, he meditated on the mystery of that divine promise: ". . . you shall be the father of a host of nations." What did those words signify? Is not every man, for his own part, the father of the future? He also told himself that the race of men was evil. The lusts of the Pentapolis scandalized his solitude, and now, he wondered whether the speech that consecrated him as "the father of future times," was not a divine curse . . .

VII

THREE young men emerged from a clump of mimosas and headed toward the oak whose foliage sheltered the meditations of the patriarch. They were similarly dressed in goatskin tunics, the hair of which was stained with the dust of the roads. Side by side, they were of equal stature, and equal beauty, and similar to such a degree that they could not be distinguished, appearing to be the personification of one another. They were of equal age and radiated with an equal intensity an ineffable adolescence. Evocative, candid and savant, their eyes fused their gazes into one alone, in an eternal flame, for a single virtue emanated from all three of them. The movements of their arms and legs were simultaneous, as if mutually regulated, generated ineluctably by one another. They progressed with a long, agile stride.

The patriarch rose to his feet. His ecstatically troubled vision unified the triple apparition and, marching to meet the three young men, he prostrated himself, face to the ground, begging: "Lord, if I have found favor in your eyes, do not pass by without seeing your slave. Repose under this tree. Wash your feet, rest your body. You can resume your route tomorrow."

With three measures of wheat flour Sara prepared cakes, and offered butter and milk.

"We are going to Sodom, and we want to reach it before nightfall."

Those words they had articulated in unison, at the same moment. Their lips had moved simultaneously, had had the same palpitation, and had made a single Voice heard.

"In Sodom, they worship Baal on the mountain of Pehor, and they also worship Kamosch; but they no longer see in Kamosch anything but the symbol of Pleasure . . ."

The celestial bloom of their faces was not sullied by a shadow. Only their eyes opened immensely over inscrutable abysms of sadness and wrath.

VIII

O N the threshold of the tent, the three
young men stood motionless. Divinized
by the crimson and gold with which the vesperal
sky glorified them, they welcomed the homage
of the setting sun.

The Voice made itself heard:

"The clamor of Sodom and Gomorrah has
multiplied and their Sin is excessively aggra-
vated. I shall descend and I shall see whether
their crime justifies that clamor, which has risen
as far as me."

Abraham, prostrating himself, asked:

"Will you doom the just with the impious?
If fifty just men are in the city, shall they perish
with the guilty? Will you not pardon that place
in favor of those fifty just men, if they are found

within it? Far be it from you to want to treat the just in the same way as the impious. That does not befit you. You, who judge the entire earth, would never execute that judgment.

THE LORD

If I find fifty just men in the city of Sodom, I shall extend my pardon over all, in their favor.

ABRAHAM

Since I have dared to undertake it, I shall speak to my Lord, I who am only dust and ash. What will you do if there are five fewer? Will you destroy the entire city, in spite of those forty-five?

THE LORD

I shall not destroy it if I find forty-five therein.

ABRAHAM

But if there are only forty, what will you do?

THE LORD

In favor of those forty. I shall not strike.

ABRAHAM

Lord, I beg you not to be indignant if I speak.
What will you do if there are only thirty?

THE LORD

If there are thirty, no harm will be done.

ABRAHAM

Since I have dared to undertake it, I will
speak to my Lord. What will you do if there are
only twenty?

THE LORD

In favor of those twenty. I shall not kill.

ABRAHAM

Lord, I beg you not to be angry if I speak once more. What will you do if there are only ten?

THE LORD

Because of those ten. I shall not destroy.

. . . And they went away, when Abraham had finished speaking.

IX

PASTORS summoned their flocks, driving to the cisterns long-haired goats, hydrocephalous rams with fleeces signed with red crosses and oxen with their muzzles extended, bellowing at the first splashes of starlight on the horizon. Descending from the slopes of Hebron, a capering slave was beating donkeys on the rump, from which enormous wineskins were dangling.

The strangers walked beneath the clusters of date-palms. Around fires launching forth red columns that set ablaze the motionless surfaces of swimming-baths, a tribe of lepers was camped. Some, crouching in their rags, were supervising the cushion of repose. The others were singing, lying down, refreshing their calcined faces with the mist of nocturnal dew. A few, amid the taciturn indifference of their brethren, were howling and rolling under the bite of the mobs of ulcers clawing their flesh; groups were unwrapping their wounds and comparing them by firelight.

The strangers advanced toward the human Dolor. At their approach the entire tribe stood up. Staffs were whirled. A clamor tore the obstructed throats: "Beware! Beware! Unclean! Unclean!" And stone cymbals clashed, struck against one another simultaneously. But before the gaze of the passers-by, the staffs fell back and the cries were stifled—and of their own accord, knees flexed under the tutelary benediction of that Gaze, which said: "You are my elect." The mewling of jackals faded away in the expanse of the night.

An impious boscage barred the route. It was planted with Asherahs. The phallic stakes arranged their offensive forms in quincunxes. A warm darkness breathed in those lubriciously marked-out avenues, channeling moisture, ferrying luxurious perfumes, ticklish laughter, weary sighs, cries and the gagged appeal of kisses. An entire city of prostitutes was celebrating the Night. Whispering shadows accumulated silently at the crossroads. Gold clinked, coins dropping one by one into the hollows of extended hands. Their robes tucked up, courtesans were wandering around pillars topped by indecent capitals. Under the beams of light raining down from the sky the pillars shone at the base, lubricated by the incessant caress of unctuous and fervent hands, and along the milky ways that the symmetrical columns prolonged, processions of adolescent Pedeschim passed, swinging their hips and laughing, directing appeals to the wooden visitors and murmured requests for golden or silver shekels.

The black triangles of tents silhouetted the outlying districts against the blue clarity of the night. Then, suddenly two gigantic statues appeared camped on their porphyry pedestals, with the heads of men and the bodies of bulls, deploying great dentellate veils from their eagle wings. The two Kerubim were facing one another at the entrance to an Assyrian palace.

X

THE strangers went to the house of Lot, the nephew of Abraham, whose house was situated near the gates of the city. Having perceived them, he got up, went to meet them and, prostrating himself before them, forehead to the ground, he worshiped them. "I beg you," he said, "to enter the house of your slave. Stay here. Wash your feet and you can resume your route tomorrow."

"Not at all," they replied. "We shall stay outside."

He turned them away from that sojourn in the city. They entered into his dwelling and ate, while he had bread baked and prepared a meal. But before they had gone to bed, the entire people, all the inhabitants of the city from children to old men, surrounded the house. They called to Lot and said to him: "Where are the men who entered your house tonight? Bring them here that we might know them."

Lot advanced toward them, after having closed the door behind him, and said to them: "Do not commit that crime, my brethren. I have two daughters who have not known men. I will bring them to you and you may abuse them in accordance with your desire, but you shall do no harm to these men, because they have entered the shade of my roof."

As they persisted, doing violence to the master of the place and threatening to irrupt therein, the strangers extended their arms and closed the door, after having brought Lot back inside the house . . .

XI

THEN the Lord considered the wall that separated him from the crowd and against which howls and a battering ram collided. The wall was effaced before the gaze of Yahveh. Over the whole extent of the square blockaded by a circular array of androphinxes, the multitude dilated its mass. Everyone was there: those who judged crimes, the priests of Baal, Kamosch and Asherah; others crowned with hyacinth, whose breasts were rutilant with pectorals studded with precious stones and whose girdles were entwined with clinking banderoles of gold; the great Sacrificers with their tiaras circled by a triple crown of electrum, with a fringe of little bells similar to the calices of henbane; Egyptian priests coiffed with staged tresses, clad in short sarraux and brandishing the heads of rams on emblematic shafts with solar disks on top. There were also bare-chested warriors with powerful bone-structures, and Assyrians with braided beards and hair streaming with scented oils, and children twisting the long knotted tresses of their temples into thongs. All ran there carrying their riches, expelled from their dwellings by the same folly, fustigated by the same lust, convulsed by the same delirium, braying under the same spurs.

Quivers ran through the masses, rippling the impatient multitude. A signal suddenly surged from an earthenware vase. Then there was a melee of jewels. The city stifling in opulence fought with its riches. The night was dazzled by flamboyances of cornelian symbolizing the blood of Isis, livid spindles ridden by emerald frogs and feldspar colonnettes, sheaves of mystical eyes bearing bites of anger and snakes, and sparkling clouds of amethyst kopirrou, obsidian and crystal scarabs, fulgurant divers of Osiris in lapis-lazuli, golden hailstones of Anubis and garnet Nephtys . . .

Launched against one another, vases shattered in explosions of perfume. Nostrils vibrant, the crowd sniffed sensual ventilations that fanaticized flesh. A whinnying of laughter burst forth frantically, twisting jaws, as bristling arms beat the air. With oscillations of intoxication, heads falling on to shoulders, a universal enlacement kneaded the substance of the crowd into a unity, and then . . . silence, a rumbling silence run through by frissons and anguished by the same breathlessness.

The sidereal lights have withdrawn. In nocturnal nature there is a pause of amazement. But on the nearer escarpments of Adamah and Zoar, volcanoes have hoisted their beacons and soaring conflagrations, pouring diluvian illuminations of blood down on the revels of Sodom.

The calm is brief. Soon, an awakening of clamors is propagated. A rage of profanations brings the crowd to its feet. "To the Sepulchers!" That cry disperses it. Exhumed from houses and temples, heavy casks are rolled. A fleet of coffins develops; sycamore hulls molded over the bodies of mummies and cutting cadavers at the neck set sail, rearing up and falling.

The multitude crouches down; the coffins are eviscerated. Out with vases full of unguents and canopic jars whose extraction allows sacred animals to fall: hawks, jackals, snakes, embalmed rats, eggs and ibises! Out with trestles of alabaster, great earthenware jars and the votive tablets of scribes! Stand up, the dead with striped faces, and head-dresses striped with black and blue! The resurrection has arrived!

The dead stand up, hands folded over breasts, clutching emblems, ansate crosses, twisted girdles, tats and garlands of ivy. They stand up like monoliths and deliver to the manipulations of the crowd the sovereign rigidity of their skin sown over perfumes. For an instant, they appear upright, swathed in metallic sheaths. Some, ringed by diadems, disinter forgotten monarchies. Helmets signaling captains are a brief commemoration of glory. Others are only opulent individuals with fingers stuffed with rings, arms circled by bracelets, clasps in the shape of scorpions, baboons and golden vultures. Their chains are conjugated from the heads of geese and their necklaces elevated ropes of flowers, pursuits of antelopes, tigers and winged cobras.

The stir of the multitude imprints the mummies with tintinnabulating oscillations. They collapse suddenly, as if suddenly scythed down, but rear up again almost immediately, stripped of their bandages, their linen and their jewels. Their nudity is passed from hand to hand. They are torn apart, mutilated, for lust has unsheathed javelins and breathed an insurmountable need to carve the flesh that has just been profaned.

But in the center of the square, wineskins are being punctured. Arms raise jars into fountains in which Engaddy and Hebron are gushing. Underfoot the ground is softening, spreading out in a winy mud that receives extenuated bodies, falling one upon another, and the snores of slumber are assimilated by the rumbling respiration of the volcanoes that are setting the nearer summits of Zoar and Adamah ablaze.

Nothing survives of the tumult but the heart-rending mewling of sacred cats. Climbing on to the roofs, brushing with the elastic paws the ledges over which their wily spines elongate, perching their sensuality on the heads of sphinxes, imploring one another on the esplanades of temples, they exchange their amorous gasps, and the sated consider, with their indifferent and luminous eyes, the swell of individuals lying in ruts of wine amid golden paving-stones and enamel tiles.

A cock sounds the day.

Immediately, the bodies, accustomed to that strident injunction, stretch, expelled by resolute and precipitate movements from the heaviness of slumber. With the same surge, the entire city stands upright. It disperses, rushing to the baths and, cleansed of the filth of the night by lustral water, it reappears, transfigured by that vivifying purification. Slaves sweep the square, effacing the shocking imprints, arranging the coffins, picking up the jewels, in which the decency commanded to their initial possessors by the light of day has preserved, for those who find them, a tranquil propriety.

The upstanding have recovered their definitive equilibrium. Physiognomies have reconquered their anterior expressions. The priests of Baal, Kamosch, and Asherah, those crowned with hyacinth, the Egyptian pontiffs and the great Sacrificers have reinstalled sacerdotal unction in their visages. Honest and circumspect, merchants blossom. All of them seem to profess a singular esteem for one another. Their eyes honor one another reciprocally and their gazes, imprinted with a mutual urbanity, forbid one another with the utmost rigor any remembrance of complicity, any frivolous allusion and any unfortunate and inconvenient memory.

Then the Angel who accompanied the Lord, addressing Lot, said: "Get up. Take your wife and two daughters and flee, in order that you do not perish in the ruination of this city."

XII

PEACE, order and respect for the laws seemed to be proclaimed by the radiant suavity of the morning. The resumption of daily labor utilized the civic and domestic duties. Oxen in long harnesses hauled under the gate of the city turreted with magadilou sleds laden with diorite and the gray granite of Ouady-Hammamat. Slaves bearing jars of wine trooped to the entrance of a wine-cellar; others, on roofs, emptied sacks of wheat through the skylights of grain-lofts. Around braziers, Phoenician artisans were blowing glass at the extremity of long tubes; alongside masons chipping bitumen, crouching Egyptians sculpted limestone in the sunlight. Caulking sycamore planks, carpenters were nailing with acacia spines the oblong lid of a mummy-case illustrated with symbolic legends. Meekly kneeling camels, their eyes wandering and benevolent, their tongues handing out between jaws ruminating leafy memories, encumbered the crossroads, awaiting burdens.

The painted faces of houses were decorated by colonnettes of colored wood. They signaled a sagely-acquired ease, civilized tastes regulated in accordance with fortune and revealing, with the desire to enchant passers-by, the premeditation of extracting therefrom a homage to the merits of the proprietor and the beautiful appearances of his "situation." The ornamentations were weighted by scientific severities or evaporated in flights of fantasy. Savant meanders mingled with rosettes, going from the heads of oxen to symmetrical flights of geese. The majority of the dwellings were solemnized by a portico of columns inhabited by statues. Avenues of date-palms and doum-palms extended through the gardens. A central naos circumscribed the intimacy of the akhonouti.

The temples were deserted by the priests as well as the people, uniquely devoted to lucrative trafficking; but their external richness, excusing the negligence of souls, was their pride and their consolation, Cryptic arrays perpetuated the pensive crouch of the androsphinxes with human heads and the bodies of lions linking the temples to one another. They rose up on columns of roseate granite

Coiffed with sistra, heads of Hathor divinized the four faces of pillars florid with lotuses, papyrus leaves, exalting on their capitals the benign blossoming of a bearded, replete BISOU,[1] bare legs parted, hands posed flat on the thighs, and above that ventripotent joviality, the mystical faces of women dreamed, pricking up heifer's ears, whose hair was plastered over the forehead by three vertical bandlets and fell back over the shoulders in a heavy woven curtain. On the facades, arborescences ramified as well as the lineaments of fluvial plants, and immutable processions were aligned of mitered hawks anchored in their augural positions, and, launching forth in grave flights of ecstasy, hieratical ibises next to birds with human arms, seated in worship on the Sign of Solemn Feasts.

Between the columns, obelisks surged. Their tips, carved into pyramids, shone with plates of bronze, electrum and gilded copper, dedicated

---

1 This word is capitalized in the original; it is now commonplace in French as a slang term for a kiss but the reference here is to a grotesque dwarfish figure in ancient Egyptian art, often described in Egyptological literature as a god.

to the sun the adorations of baboons and sac-
rifices to Ra-Harmakis whose pious representa-
tions sanctified the pedestal of the monument.
Statues were backed against the walls, and at
their feet projected stone ledges, the tables of
offering on which were exposed loaves of bread,
the thighs of oxen and vases of libations.

Those temples were closed. Their heavy
doors, sealed over the rubble of their intimate
deserts, permitted the magnificences of their
exterior architecture to be admired.

XIII

MEANWHILE, the crowd, of its own accord was flocking to the passage of Yahveh: the whole crowd, from children to old men, the same crowd that the cockcrow had so briskly extracted from the extenuation of its pleasures. A halt was made to all negotiation and all labor. The artisans deserted their tools; the conductors their sleds and their teams; the slaves the cellars and the grain-lofts; the Phoenician glassblowers their braziers; the masons their bitumen; the Egyptians their limestone; the carpenters their sycamore hulls. They ran in enthusiastic, maddened, possessed, turbulent bands, acclaiming the tracks of the Stranger. The houses were emptied of their inhabitants. At the head of the multitude he walked, drawing all the life of the city. He marched without appearing to hear the footfalls of the formidable troop that was escorting him.

"Salut to the nabi! Tell us, then, words of wisdom! Sing us songs of glory! The future! The future! Ah! Tell us the future! The things of tomorrow!"

Indifferent to the obsessive solicitations that were buzzing in his ears, the Stranger, ravishing human wills, wrapped them in the sovereign current of his divinity. In his wake, the people scaled the heights of the city . . .

XIV

THEY have spread out over the entire plain. They are blackening the chalky immensity of the plateau that dominates the fields and crowns the hierarchical terraces. The fortifications round out their mistrustful cliffs.

Beyond, what transporting beauties of the landscape! What a heart-warming valor of blissful vegetation! In God's garden what a pious competition of embellishment! Vision sets sail over the fields of the Salty Sea, the marvelous fields extending to infinity, very calm, splashing and rippling in the sunlight! On the shores, the solemnities of mountains of sepulchral crypts, the supercilious statuary of rocks, the adventurous tips of promontories, the aquatic hostelries of gulfs. On the banks, the grassy fertility of vegetation, the jubilant glare of fluvial plants, the youth of laurels in rosy dress, the alluvial nobility of crimson poplars, the preponderancies of aquiliary trees, thickets of aloes in gala dress, the hieroglyphic clustering of reeds. Down below, on watch, an entire archipelago of cormorants. The holy frolics of marabouts; projections ripping the surface, some are asleep or meditating dogmatically on the vertical stick of one paw, necks pulled back. Others are shivering with great wing-beats, shedding fine down. There are immutable ones that, plumage bristling, consider the water despairingly. Enthusiastic assemblies whose whiteness is brooding ecstasy point their beaks at the sky and dedicate to the culminating serenities their nostalgia of ascension. With long, measured steps the solitaries among them perambulate, exploring the thickets. And amicable breezes pass over that blossoming of water, earth, plants, flowers and birds.

XV

AT the feet of Yahveh the oceanic multitude immobilizes in an impartial attention. A breath of fervor is exhaled by the souls present. One would think that they were congregated by a curiosity doubtless unconscious but surely praiseworthy. One could believe that they had hastened to see some unspeakably edifying spectacle.

The visages are cleansed to such an extent of the soiling of the previous night that they appear to have conquered a new identity. Above all, they reveal a beautiful health of the soul, just as they express the fruitful cultivation of the body. Ossified by reason, clad in a fraudulent candor, their expression only differs in its nuances, in its subtlest reflections. August, austere or frivolous, they brazenly affirm for one another a consideration based on respective merits. Some have a magnanimous bearing. The majority are reflective, as ponderous as could be wished, exhibiting a tangibly advanced maturity. All display an incorruptible integrity, an impeccable rectitude, so bravely honest, so splendidly irrepressible, so scrupulously just and so cordially generous that they appear to be armed against any dissidence, resolute with the most supreme rigor against the reproofs of Opinion.

Each visage emanates an expert gaze, which seems to evaluate the importance of the Personage proposed so spontaneously to their benevolent appreciation. The "sympathetic interest" that they had awarded primitively to God seems irrational to them. The appearances of the Sovereign Master are "not liable to conciliate him to the regard of the crowd." His apparel—"perhaps neglected"—denotes a suspect irregularity of existence, an incontinence of thought, independent mores, an eccentricity devoid of premeditation, an elevation without measure, an unadmitted disinterest, an unbridled passion, immediately extending to the Grand, to the Good and the Beautiful and laying siege to the Ideal.

Occult prevaricators, masked concussionaries, simoniacs farded with virtue, artists traitorous to art, thinkers trafficking Thought, disloyal artisans, falsifying merchants, vendors of spirit, vendors of soul and vendors of flesh: All Sodom is assembled there in an exceedingly fraternal, exceedingly discreet communion of Sin. By virtue of preliminary observation, whispered to one another, All Sodom is disposed to pronounce a definitive judgment on the intellectual and moral value of the Almighty.

XVI

FIRST, there was a recitation of the funeral celebrations in commemoration of the death of Adonis in the distant lands where Moloch and Ashtoreth are worshiped, at Byblos. For seven days the city had roared. Mobs of women, in search of the Image, beat the squares and the streets, passing like gusts of wind, tearing their hair and ripping their garments, stimulating the fervor of the people with their howls of carnivorous beasts: "Aï Adonai! Aï Adonai!" The mortuary flute spread out in tears. Among the Amalechites, it was Urotal and Lilith; among the Arameans Hadad-Melek and Ehyun: everywhere, temples of pleasure; everywhere, altars of flesh; everywhere, the Adored Beast! Nowhere the Lord, the only Omnipotent God!

For an instant, the Voice appears to collapse in a gulf of bitterness.

It springs forth from the depths and soars above the crowd; it bursts forth in the mysterious tempests of its wrath:

"Queen in the land of Canaan, on the day of your birth, the cord that links you to your mother is not cut. You have not been plunged into the salutary water. You were not enveloped in linen. On the day of your birth, you were projected on to the face of the earth, you were crushed in abjection."

A smile embellishes the painted lips and, rejoicing the eyes darkened with antimony, propagates "interest" throughout the audience. Exchanged glances declare themselves amused by the Word of God. Some, however, are alarmed by intimate anxieties. Some expressions have rung false: "the cord that links you to your mother" . . . ought one not to fear more indecent audacities? And then, is it not going to be lachrymose? But they are reassured. Doubtless that initial sadness is only an ingenious feint. It is going to cheer up. It is proceeding, via unfamiliar detours, toward palpitating or graciously jovial recitations.

The Voice:

"I have cleansed you of your blood. I have rubbed you with oil. I have dressed you in purple and shod you in hyacinth. I have given a diadem to your forehead, bracelets to your arms, rings to your fingers, necklaces to your neck—and your name has gone forth, rebounding from nation to nation, because of your beauty, for you were edified in my Splendor and, proud of the Splendor that I have put into you, you have prostituted yourself . . ."

At that word, a unanimous, indulgent and premonitory rumor reprimands the divine voice and, recalling it to decency, forbids it deviations of language that its apparent indignation could not justify. The audience has not applied the formal accusations with an increasing anger. It only suffers from the imminent coarseness of the Lord.

". . . And you have displayed your prostitution to all passers-by in order that all passers-by might soil your flesh . . ."

Fanatical protests reprove that new and licentious crudity.

The Voice:

"At all the crossroads you have affixed the sign of your prostitution, and you have prostituted yourself as has never been done before and will never be done again. You have prostituted yourself with the sons of the Egyptians and you were not satisfied. You have prostituted yourself with the sons of the Assyrians and you were not satisfied. In the land of Canaan, with the Chaldeans, you have multiplied your fornications . . ."

Again! This time, the Opinion of men has been too insolently challenged. It seems that the Sal-Aphot of the Libyan deserts has just blown its incendiary gusts over the faces. Pudorized cheeks turn red. The eyelids of Sodom are lowered shamefully.

"You have wallowed in debauchery in the public squares . . ."

From one end of the audience to the other, long vociferations overlap. His modesty exasperated, a Pausaire, one of those who regulate the halts in processions of Isis, waves his arms and addresses God:

"You are not able, then," he clamors, "to distract our minds without wounding our ears? Your hymns delight us, but your words offend us. Our ears want to be respected."

The Voice:

"You have torn away the insignia of splendor, the signs of gold and silver that I had given you and you have fabricated masculine images with them to which you have prostituted your-selves . . ."

"Out of the city, obscene speech-maker! Out with the nabi! Unclean! Unclean!"

With a loud explosion, the modest revolt of the crowd is vulcanized. Vengeful javelins are brandished above obfuscated heads. Arrows are launched in a radiant rain. Stones fall like hail. The mob of the virtuous howls canticles of extermination.

The entire people, from children to old men, the same people who surrounded the house of Lot and who demanded the divine visitors for their own pleasure, those same people rush against God, push him toward the exit from the city and, having expelled him, close the gates again victoriously, glorifying themselves in that sanitizing execution.

XVII

YAHVEH climbed the neighboring mountain. His anger no longer rose up at the thought of monstrous lusts. He proclaimed that the modesty of Sodom was the true, the unforgivable, crime of the city.

The people, watching, booed the ascension of the God whose speech had scandalized them. Suddenly, the people fell, face downwards. They had just seen the Arm extended over the volcanoes that were flamboyant on the nearer escarpments of Zoar and Adamah.

THE GUARDIAN SHADES

Love is a spiritual conjunction. It follows that all those who are in the spiritual world are associated in accordance with their amours; here it is the same.

Emmanuel Swedenborg,
On the New Jerusalem.

ONLY the relatives remained in the drawing room, and the expansive cordiality
died away in a mistrustful silence.

"If you wish, we can occupy ourselves with
questions of interest."

Those simple words had quieted the joviality
of conversations imperatively, and before the
fireplace with massive andirons, the old man
who had just pronounced that invitation to
silent readiness, prepared to speak. With stipu-
latory words and judicious gestures, moving his
forearms, his fingers folded, only the thumb upright or the elbows parted, his palms flat, like an
officiant at the Preface, sometimes toying with
the coral cask swinging on his watch-chain, he
drew closer to one another those he named as
future and dear spouses. They both listened

with an avid attention. Their gazes, accustomed for half a century to smile with a familiar affection, seemed, in their suspicious and defensive reserve, to anticipate the imminence of a conflict. When they met, interrogatively, they had never scrutinized their reciprocal pupils so disobligingly, and they assigned to one another a citatory animosity before the competence of the mediator whose eyelids were delighting in knowing winks.

Colloquia were engaged in an unusual idiom. Unfamiliar terms—bearer bonds, transfers, consolidated shares, coupons, usufruct—caught fire in the exquisite sadness of the old drawing room. Evaluations of immovable property and estimations of superficiality chagrined the light peace that embalmed the faded memory of a pastoral century. The term "preferential legacy" astonished as it brushed the mother's lips. The father riposted with a "paraphernal argument" The memory was exhumed of a "nuncupative testament" and the old man, whose eyes caressed the fragmentary berquinades running over the doors, talked about liquidating a community of which the generous combination affected his professional scruples. Then, the arbiter having pronounced: "That constitutes, then, save for interior modifications, the bases of the imminent contract," faces cleared and a rejoicing of tender smiles celebrated the return of the interrupted abandons.

Outside the window, an avenue of tall plane trees filed in a long trail of shadow, outlined against the distant orifice of clarity that the avenue opened to the daylight, the double silhouette of the fiancés. The mother parted the curtains and, allowing two tears to fall that had arrived at the extremities of her lashes, pronounced: "Look—we have no need to hear them to know whether they're happy!"

Under the ceiling of foliage, Marcelle and Henri were walking side by side with a pensive slowness. The radiant Sunday afternoon was dreaming piously. The plain deployed its extent without a frisson: there was no head and shoulders of an ox-herd emerging from the swell of long grass, his eyes extended over the furrows between the horns of his oxen, nor the ardent parabola of spades, nor the swarming of livestock, nor the shrill complaints of spinning shepherdesses pointing the lances of their distaffs cravated with wool and making spindles pirouette: nothing. The fields propagated their bushy immobility and progressed in the stagnation of extinct gold over which the autumn rounded out an orb of limpid azure, criss-crossed by the flight of the last swallows. The mountains were also cloaked in a Sabbath silence. At the exit from the path, sleepy ponds glittered in the sunlight and the bells that were ringing vespers crowded the air with sighing prayer.

To either side, the colonnades of old trees erected their obelisks decorated with hiero-glyphs, dates and symbolically-enlaced names. Ingenuous hearts, perpetuated by the sap, scarred their wounds, or reappeared, half-effaced, under flakes of burst bark. Infused with the life of the trees, some swelled with monstrous hypertrophy. Others were anemic, atrophying with old age, no longer marking their ragged contours with anything but a line of rust, and the centenarian pillars of that commemorative crypt sent those mementos of amour to one another.

Designating a stone bench, reddened like the platform of a dolmen, Henri asked: would you like to sit down, Marcelle?"

She acquiesced with a nod of the head and, gathering up her dress, she sat down next to him. A comparison of their features established an almost consanguineous synonymy between them: the same appearance of age—still adolescent—the same suavity of soul in the expression of their delicate faces, signed by the ideal; and the same contemplative ardor in their eyes. The flame in the depths of the young woman's eyes was, however, more intense. More active and softer, with the fixed glare of a pendant lamp, her gaze retreated beneath the arches of her eyebrows. Darkened by the brim of her straw hat, her forehead diminished monastically, enclosed by the black tresses of her hair, and a drop of shadow trembled on her lip.

The rumble of a carriage made them turn their heads simultaneously toward the path, and, recognizing the alert old man who had just presided over the discussion of respective interest, Henri murmured: "So we're betrothed, by the will of our families." Then, compressing his temples between his fingers: "Listen, Marcelle, everything that has just been said between our parents, you can divine. They've resolved our marriage. They've doubtless fixed the epoch, impatient to realize what they believe to be our happiness. They haven't consulted us, unable to anticipate the slightest resistance on our part to their dearest and most just desire. Well, Marcelle, I ought to tell you, and I am telling you, without fear, since our childhood authorizes me to speak to you as to a sister, that it is necessary for our relatives to renounce what they want to accomplish. I cannot tell you that I would be sure of happiness with you, sure of our happiness. You also know that fortune matters little to me. In any case, will not our disinterest make us as rich as one another? I am separated from you by a promise made to myself alone, in the secrecy of my soul. I am engaged."

Without seeing it, he sensed the young woman's gaze become blissful, and their souls were penetrated by such a lucid intuition that he discerned in the tremor that agitated her the shudder of a supreme joy.

Then as they looked one another in the eyes, transfigured by an evocative ecstasy, he said: "The woman I love is a foreigner, a Spaniard, or perhaps an Italian. Her name is Maria . . . simply Maria. She is as beautiful as you, but she does not have, like you, the gaze or the voice of a sister. She has the beauty of an apparition. Her face is one of those that pass through dreams, one of those before whom, while asleep, it seems to us that we are kneeling, arms open, lips extended, and who are considering us, without moving, and always smiling . . ."

Marcelle's eyes were wonderstruck with an equal enthusiasm and, interrogating him, she asked: "Do you think you will see her again?"

"See her again? See her again . . . !" He put his hands together. For a few moments, his gaze was immobilized, desperately, staring at the line of the horizon. Then he shook his head and murmured: "I don't know . . . I want to die in that hope. I saw her at the theater in Bordeaux, in my first and only emergence from the house. It seemed to me that we had known one another for a very long time and were finding one another again after a very long voyage. She was surrounded by white-haired gentlemen who called her Maria and opened tortoiseshell candy-boxes in front of her. They addressed her as '*tu*' . . . doubtless relatives. But her eyes were fixed on me, ink-black eyes that seemed to grow when one contemplated them, and she smiled at me, so pale, her lips parted, without a movement. Her arm was posed on the edge of the box and I saw that she had a golden bracelet, without reflection, closed by a green stone—a malachite, I think . . . My God! To see her again . . . !

"What does it matter; my thought is able to find her again, and I'm sure that, in spite of the distance, surely insurmountable, that separates us, I am close to her, as she is close to me . . . Thus, we love one another and are betrothed."

Marcelle had lowered her eyelids. Twisting around her fingers the tuft of red ribbons knotted around the handle of her umbrella, she sighed: "I too am betrothed. Like you, I believe, I'm sure, that he is thinking about me. It was in that voyage I made to Marseille with Maman last year. I saw him on the deck of a steamer. We looked at one another for a long time and I sensed that he was the only man I could love. All the sadness that there was in his pallor seemed to dissipate at the sight of me, and as he drew away his eyes remained attached to mine. Someone shouted: 'Paul!' With the tips of his fingers he threw a kiss into the air which he might have addressed to the land, but which I took for myself alone. Alas, shall I ever see him again . . . ?"

Less exuberant in expression than Henri's, that deploring question quivered in the pain-racked depths of her exceptional soul. A silence was interposed. Then Marcelle, blushing, making her voice firm, which she sensed about to weaken at every word, she pronounced: "It is your sister of childhood who is . . . begging you, Henri. Our parents will die of dolor if we refuse . . ."

"It's impossible, Marcelle. We cannot give one another what others have taken from us."

"We can marry our sadness," she proposed. "We can love one another as we can, in the thought of the absentees and in the fidelity that we will always retain for them."

"I shall never forget her!" he cried.

"All my life belongs to him," she swore.

She removed her hand from her glove and extended it with such a radiant prayer that he let his own fall, sobbing the name: "Maria." He kissed the young woman's forehead, and her lips murmured, with the fervor of a consecration to eternal suffering: "Paul . . . to you alone . . . forever . . ."

The bells of distant churches were now ringing the carillons of the *magnificat*, and their triumphant volleys, which sublimated the air with their alleluias, exalted that candid ordination, the bold renunciation that they dedicated to the essence of imperishable sentiments.

The solitude in which they cloistered their existence hermetically fortified their individual contemplation. The house was, moreover, identified with their introversion by virtue of the sadness that it exhaled, not in the currents of chilly air sighing in the ruins, but in that subtle dust, that volatilization of perfumed atoms emanating from elegances of yore. Their eyes were ignorant there of the tinsel fantasies of furniture flagrant with the present. The things that surrounded them were the disparate survivors of abolished luxury, but the melancholically dilapidated expression of their original grace inspired a retrospective tenderness and made death lovable.

At the intersection of two paths, the manor was turning gray in the aquatic verdure of its moats and beneath the landslides of shadow that flowed from the enormous rump of the mountain. In the courtyard, traversed at determined intervals by a maidservant carrying an earthenware pitcher balanced on a turban, peacocks were dirtying the sparkling train of their plumage, cocks were pawing the ground, and pilgrim ducks were steering their processions toward respected cloacas. Crouching on the pillars of the gate, plaster lions were yawning. Inside, the rooms were multiplied, opening on tiled corridors. They were ceilinged with high wood paneling and the windows hollowed out profound cells in the walls. Sheets of twisted wool suspended villanelles. Four-poster beds, beds with tents and beds with baldaquins, dust-covers and imperials occupied the corners. On the mantelpieces, empire clocks edified marble parthenons. Smoky pastels commemorated bucolic enjoyments on the apple-green carpets of bowling greens. Miniatures framed parliamentary faces strictly garroted by cravats with multiple turns; and a red chalk drawing caricatured a card-player calculating the chances of an *écart*, crushed beneath the hull of his French hat. It was the work of an unknown artist, a guest welcomed in the days when the house had opened its gates to passers-by on the road.

Among those relics of defunct epochs, Henri and Marcelle acclimatized their dreams to the hospitality of their sadness. Each of them, with a tacit accord, was doubled. Beside each of them lived an occult being who, for them, affirmed a real presence. Their words seemed indirect and their gazes, which never weighed upon one another, instinctively scrutinized their vicinity and animated the apparent void that surrounded them. For one another they had a fraternal regard and they associated their amity in the private cult that they consecrated to their elect.

At meal times—the only ones, along with late evenings, that could distract them from the thoughtful silence they cherished—they interested their illusions in their placid conversation. The phrases that they exchanged were not expressed for their exclusive profit. They were underlined by intentions, the transparent fervor of which inspired pale smiles and pensively tearful sighs. The names of those they loved were never pronounced between them. Would not naming them have been to deny them? And when the insistent solicitations of their thought saddened their joviality, they sequestered themselves in a similar abstraction, their elbows on the arms of their armchairs, face to face, before the dying embers of the fire. And thus their affection, far from cooling, was knotted more indissolubly in the parallel and inviolate union of their sentiments.

Scaling the mountains in the huntress dawns of autumn, roaming the plains calcined by the sun when the torpors of summer weighed down the flight of quail in the buckwheat, Henri enjoyed the radiant society of Maria. In the depths of the woods, in the night of foliage, where invisible springs sang and doves cooed, he evoked her with a sovereign arrogance, and the enchantments that penetrated him forbade him, as despicable and deceptive, to wish for the reality.

But it was in the soul of Marcelle, above all, that the obsession took root. Less prompt in imagination, her contemplation was illuminated by more certain clairvoyances. Of a mystic race, meditation, always launched in prayer toward the defined object, created a sufficient activity for her; and she felt enlaced with that inseparable companion by bonds more unbreakable than the derisory enchainment sealed by precarious magistrates.

In the hangars of the courtyard she had discovered, nested amid the rubble, an abandoned chapel, doubtless dating from an immemorial epoch. The stone slabs that formed a tumulary checkerboard repeated *hic jacets* and *transiturs*, with effaced names and corroded dates. A blazoned bronze plaque remained incrusted in the dust on the stone of the altar. Into that altar disinherited of worship, Marcelle had reintegrated the primitive consecration, for she had made it the refuge of a prayer whose purity her amour could not adulterate.

She also explored the house in search of things of the past. A cupboard full of lace exhaling a dying odor of iris caused her inexpressible delights, for there were instinctive affinities between her soul and those ideal fabrics. With tender precautions she laid out the vaporous cloths, the Alençons, the Argentans, the Bruxelles, the Solemn Venetians, the fans of "king's thumbs," the frivolous ruffs, the clerical guipures, the sacerdotal chrisom-cloths and rochets of Malines and Genoa bequeathed by a missionary prelate, the Archbishop of Persepolis. She threw those gauzes over her head, rolled them around her neck, put them on like albs, twisted them into scarves and, marching with a lighter step, she smiled her dazzling reflection in the depths of mirrors, in that baptismal whiteness.

Their life was gradually isolated from all external agitation. Ecstasy was radiant in their immersed faces and around them, in the mute society of cherished shades, the guardian angels of their humanity. Neighboring society had circumscribed the château with a leprosy of mystery, and no visitor any longer came through the gate of the courtyard. Frightened by influences of which they could not divine the nature, the young servants decamped; only a miserly and taciturn aged couple remained.

Grave lawsuits extracted Henri from the meditative serenity jealously enclosed within the walls of the manor. Summoned by imperious convocations, he was obliged to resolve himself to long absences. As the day fixed for his departure drew nearer, his expectation tormented him with an indefinable impatience and an anguish made of confused presentiments. It was his first excursion into life, his first escape from the spiritual perimeter that enabled him to cherish—with the affectionate company of Marcelle—the creature whose incomparable ideality he had appropriated. He was familiar with the veridical charm of the natal solitude and he was suspicious of the outside, the unexplored atmosphere that blockaded his domain and thickened, for him, well before the horizon.

Squeezing Henri's hands at the moment of the separation, Marcelle pronounced, in a voice that was struggling with tears: "You'll write to us, won't you?"

He shuddered. It was the first time that she had defined the demarcation of their existences and had pronounced the irrevocable union of her own with the woman of his thought.

He responded with a mute sign to the interrogative smile with which she accentuated her words—and as the carriage rolled along the high road he watched the silhouette of the young woman melt into the astral pallor that, amid the nocturnal obscurity, outlined like a phosphoric archipelago the cluster of towers fusing the mass of the roofs.

On his return from his first voyage, when he leapt down in the courtyard from the phaeton that he was driving, Marcelle, suddenly nonplussed, suppressed the fraternal impulse that pushed her toward him; but before she was able to extract herself from his arms, he gripped her in a wild excess of passion.

"Oh, Marcelle, my dear wife," he repeated, "how happy I am to see you again!"

Immediately, he talked about the unimaginable result of his negotiations.

"Our lawsuit has finally been won! And it was not, I assure you, slender interests that were at stake! All of the legitimate succession of the intestate reverts to us in its totality. It is millions that are falling to us. Oh, our life is going to change. How sad it is here!"

He had taken Marcelle in his arms and he felt the young woman's fingers go cold and tremble on his wrist. She considered him with an unspeakable alarm. It was not a transformation but a denaturation that had taken place in him. A youth, no longer radiant with the effusions of thought, a muscular strength, an irruption of blood, had sacked the anterior candor. That pillage of the soul, joyfully proclaimed, had laid it bare. In vain she searched beside him for the familiar shade of Maria, and the strange gaiety that she sensed vibrating in him suggested to her the impression, simultaneously cruel and trivial, of the coarsely premature rejoicing of widowhood.

"Oh, yes," he went on, "our life is going to change! I'm going, without delay, to take measures to restore our house appropriately. You'll inspire my work. You'll choose the decorations yourself. I want our architects and our furnishers to realize all your fantasies. Truly, voyages are useful, as much for the health as the mind. It's good to steep oneself in life again . . ."

Then taking the hands that she abandoned to him inertly: "Your days must have passed very sadly in this isolation?"

She recoiled, almost violently, and in a voice that strove to master a tremor of anger, she emphasized: "*We* were thinking of you."

An immediate stupor suppressed his jubilation. But he did not linger in that chagrined impression by which his good humor had been momentarily disconcerted, and, laughing, as if at the memory of an amusing adventure, he cried: "What! You have not yet awakened from your dream? You're still living in your clouds! Oh, I understand . . . it's necessary for you to travel, as I have just done myself. It's the infallible remedy for those sorts of affections. It's only by mingling with the movement of cities that one can comprehend the boring sterility of reveries in one place."

"And the scorn of oaths," she declared, with such a profundity of bitterness that she shivered involuntarily.

But a new faith transported him; a brutal will armed him against all objection, and he shrugged his shoulders: "Puerilities! Extravagances of sentiment! The true oath, the one that it is necessary to keep, we have made to the law. We have made it to God, who commands us to love one another in accordance with the heart and in accordance with reason. I don't want to know any other. We are already very culpable for having misunderstood the happiness that he had placed within the reach of our desires. It is to blaspheme against life only to love phantoms! And what is the creature that I pursued in a dream with such a ridiculous adoration? That hallucination was prolonged far too long. Now I protest against it with all the revolt of my youth. I have the right to love you, Marcelle, and I shall defend that right, even against your thought . . ."

The young woman's upper body oscillated in the breath of that growling passion. Her pallor begged for mercy and the misted gleam of her eyes revealed mental confusion.

He had drawn closer. With an impatient gaze he caressed her idealized features, solidifying their serious weave. The particularities of a beauty previously unknown were revealed, one by one, in drops of enchantment, and, so close to her ear that he made the curls of her delicate hair flutter, he murmured: "We shall be happy. Life will become beautiful in order to receive us. Let us belong to one another . . ."

His arm rounded out about Marcelle's waist, but before that pressure could bend her over her hips, she had straightened up with an irresistible effort. Upright, her pupils fixed and deserted by her gaze, she designated beside her the void from which, for her, the guests had disappeared, and, putting a finger over her lips, she marched toward her bedroom with a sure slowness.

※

She tried to pray but, disorientated, her prayer did not go to God. It bifurcated half way, galloping toward the one who finally had to come running, to manifest himself, to break the mutism whose persistence would now be an undeniable treason.

"The shades are not perjurers."

A start of fear lifted her up on her bed. Was it her who, somnolent, had murmured that response to the supplication of her thought? That consolatory phrase—she acquired a more precious certainty of that with every passing second—had been whispered by lips other than her own.

She had, moreover, felt the warmth of a breath, and something like the touch of a feathery hand on her eyelids. Then her soul expanded, magnified in its belief. He was beside her; his presence had revealed him to her. A nuptial vision illuminated her eyes. The chamber radiated whiteness, vaporizing the lace that clouded their ecstasy, and he was on his knees, having arrived from distant countries, passing gloriously through the dangers of the distance, running from the extremities of the world, because in the reflection of his soul he had seen tears flowing from the eyes that he adored him.

The wedding was celebrated. And they were alone, forgetting, in the first minute of their isolation, the mute sufferings of separation.

She looked around, smiling at the things that surrounded her—but the creak of a floorboard shook her with an abrupt shudder. Immediately, she felt the anguish of a nearby peril. Her eyes suddenly de-scaled, had dispersed the vision with a single glance.

Her ears pricked, she perceived the slide of a footstep, an arrest stifled in the exterior door-curtains. She divined hesitations, and then the march resumed, groping, finally fading away in the distance of the corridors. A stormy silence was engulfed in her brain, breathing burning currents of air there, shattering ideas, unleashing turbulent phantasmagorias, colliding with the walls of her temples, opening abysms, shaking partitions, immobilizing in a continuous moan.

Two faces passed back and forth before her without her, although having recognized them, being able to disentangle their personal identity. Two names also awoke her eardrums, singing their syllables without her being able to adapt to those obsessive appellations the two individuals that they designated, and, fixed in the blaze of her body, at the surface chilled by moisture, she listened to the tumult of her arteries, which resounded like the beating of hammers striving to demolish her reason.

"Are you suffering, Marcelle? I've consulted the doctor, who has reassured me completely. A general weakness and a slight anemia consequent on a lack of prolonged activity. He has prescribed fortifying agents, and above all a mental treatment: distractions, laughter, movement; everything that has been lacking until now. I shall supervise the observation of that regime myself. You'll be very docile, won't you?

It's necessary for you to recover your strength, that you be cured without delay."

He turned his gaze toward her. Her slender hand was clutching the mantilla of white lace that was wrapped around her neck and she was walking beside him, smiling with an expression of childish gaiety.

"Good!" he exclaimed, his eyes shining with tears of joy. "You're smiling! It's the sunshine! The bad days are over. We're going to be happy, you'll see. Don't you feel an impatience to see new lands . . . ? No, you can't, yet . . . you don't know . . . and it's my fault, for it's me who is culpable, but you'll forgive me, Marcelle; I shall invent prodigies in order to merit your pardon."

He had stopped, incapable of going on, immobilized by happiness. He looked at the surroundings as if he were inviting things to the extraordinary enjoyment that was bounding within him. The young woman tore up stems of wild oats, which she carefully gathered together, and which she decapitated, laughing, with a sudden sweep of her hand.

"As soon as you've recovered," he declared, "in a few weeks, or a few days, we'll leave for

Nice. Come, Marcelle, let's sit down, let's talk about us, only us; let's make plans . . ."

Radiant, he drew her toward the stone bench on which they had sealed with an oath the betrothals of their thought. An October afternoon was reddening over the fields. A band of "searchers" dispersed among the vines was moving between the stocks, gleaning the clotted grapes forgotten on the branches. The air was quivering with the rustle of foliage and resounding with the piping of migrating birds flying westwards in angular convoys.

He had taken the young woman's hand, pressing the fingers one by one. She uttered a slight cry of surprise and, drawing Henri's wedding-ring toward her, she examined the symbol curiously. He removed the ring and put it in Marcelle's hand with a smiling complaisance. "And your clothes?" he asked. "Have you thought about them? I want them to be marvelous. I want the people who see you to be fascinated and I shall only be truly happy when they're jealous of me."

Without responding, she considered the gold ring attentively, drowning it in a ray of sunlight running through the high branches, and all her thought extended with an ardent fixity toward that particle of metal scintillating in her fingertips.

To begin with, he had not noticed that silence. He felt so completely happy himself that he had only seen in the attitude of the young woman the expression of a charmed meditation. Even her distraction had delighted him, like a coquetry of confession agitated like a fan before the blush of an emotion. But the singular obstinacy of that mutism disconcerted his exultation.

"You're not saying anything?" he pronounced, squeezing Marcelle's arm affectionately. "Has what I've just said displeased you?"

He sensed a protestation. She did not reply. She did not even appear to feel Henri's hand, which was now bruising her flesh, the phalanges contrasted by an anxious clench. She lowered her head, bring her eyes closer to the ring, as if to decipher an illegible inscription, and she expressed a supreme projection of all her will, a desperate concentration of her reflection in the resolution of an insoluble problem.

With a feverish gesture, he wiped away the sweat that was flooding his forehead. A terrible anguish gripped his heart

"Marcelle," he begged. "Answer me!"

She rotated the wedding-ring slowly, trying to read the circular inscription. Leaning closer to her ear, he accentuated, with the decisive clarity of an injunction: "Marcelle, look at me!"

No quiver disturbed her attention. He heard her spell out, in a distinct murmur: "*H-e-n-r-i-Paul.*" She clapped her hands. Convulsions of joy shook her, making her stamp her feet, and suddenly, putting her arms around Henri, throwing her lips, burning with fever, toward the lips that recoiled, she sobbed: "Paul, it's you, Paul . . . my life . . . my only love . . ." She tried to draw him toward her, to bring him to his feet, to transport him in her delirium . . .

"Come on, then, my Paul . . . let's go . . . straight ahead . . . into the clouds . . . the other is going to come . . . the one that I hate . . . follow me . . ." And, reassembling her skirts, she drew away, still shouting, her voice intoxicated by folly.

He watched her flee like a mist over the grass. He listened to the irrevocable dementia of the laughter that was fading away in the depths of the avenue, and he almost laughed himself, so much was he suffering.